GRAY WOLF'S SEARCH

7th
GENERATION

SUMMERTOWN, TENNESSEE

by Bruce Swanson

illustrated by Gary Peterson

Gray Wolf was happy to be a member of the Wolf clan living on the northwest coast. The sea, the shore and the forest gave his people all they needed.

Looking over a fallen log, Gray Wolf saw one of his family's woolly dogs.

"Tonight I will meet with my uncle," he said to the dog happily.

"He will give me guidance for my future."

2

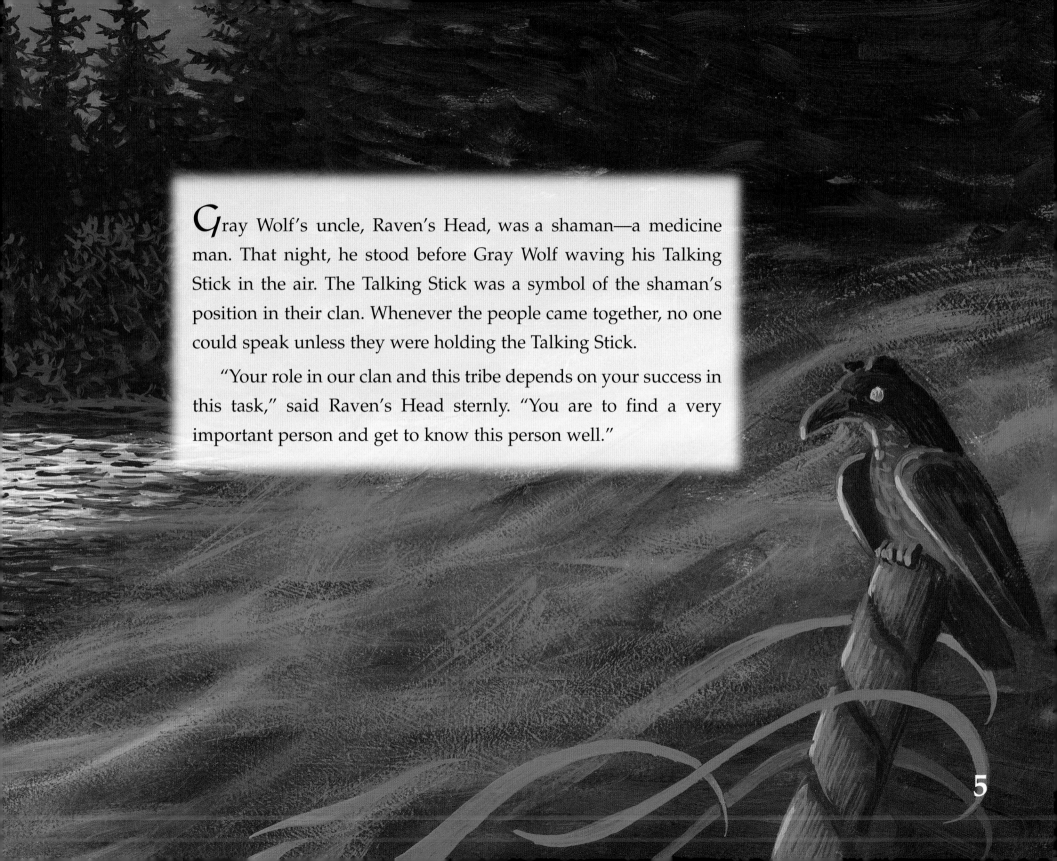

Gray Wolf's uncle, Raven's Head, was a shaman—a medicine man. That night, he stood before Gray Wolf waving his Talking Stick in the air. The Talking Stick was a symbol of the shaman's position in their clan. Whenever the people came together, no one could speak unless they were holding the Talking Stick.

"Your role in our clan and this tribe depends on your success in this task," said Raven's Head sternly. "You are to find a very important person and get to know this person well."

As Gray Wolf began his search, he came across a mother bear and her two cubs.

"Hello, Sister Bear," he said. "My uncle has told me to look for a very important person. Since you are wise with age, I wonder if you have seen such a person?"

"We bear do not have much to do with humans," she kindly replied. "I have seen a fair number in my time, but I wouldn't say that any appeared more important than the others."

"Thank you," said Gray Wolf, a little disappointed. "May you and your cubs enjoy peace and good health."

When the summer approached, Gray Wolf saw a pod of killer whales and he swam out to talk to them.

"Brother Whale," he called out. "I am looking for a very important person. Can you help me?"

"We have seen many people from many tribes," said the elder whale. "Some of your people are great hunters and fishers, but they all look and sound very much alike."

"You swam a great distance," the whale continued. "Would you like a ride back to shore?"

8

Gray Wolf grabbed the whale's high dorsal fin and climbed up excitedly. The whale carried him far out into the ocean before returning him safely to shore.

"Thanks, Brother Whale," said Gray Wolf, as he hurried back to his village to tell the story of his wonderful ride.

That fall, Gray Wolf saw a bald eagle gliding above the river.

"How is Sister Eagle this fine day?" asked Gray Wolf.

"My family and I are well, thank you," answered Eagle.

"I am looking for a very important person. Have you seen one in your far travels?"

"It is true that I cover great distances and see a great deal. But I wouldn't know an important person if I saw one."

10

"That is exactly how I have felt," said Gray Wolf.

"I wish you luck," said Eagle as she flew off. Gray Wolf began to wonder if he would ever complete his task.

11

Late in winter Gray Wolf came across a beaver family working on their lodge. "I am sorry to see that your home was ruined by the flooding," called Gray Wolf.

"It often needs repair during the rainy season," replied Beaver.

"The rainy season can last for months. You must have great patience," noted Gray Wolf.

"No more than you, I expect," said the beaver with a slap of his tail. "You would probably do the same for your family."

"I am in search of a very important person," said Gray Wolf. "Maybe you have seen one."

"I have seen none more important than you," said Beaver as he paddled away.

Looking around, Gray Wolf saw a way to help the hard-working family. He grabbed a tree the beavers had chewed off and pushed it out into the water for them.

As spring approached, Gray Wolf was gathering herbs for Raven's Head. A slight movement caught his attention and he turned his head quickly. Peering out of the dense forest were two wolves. This was good medicine. Never before had he seen the animal for which he had been named. "I am honored that you allowed me to see you," said Gray Wolf, gratefully.

The two wolves did not speak for a long time. Finally one of them said, "You are my brother. And we are both unique. I know that you have stayed true to your task. Return to your village. The time you hope for is near." Then, silently, Gray Wolf's animal relations seemed to melt into the forest.

14

The trees and flowers began to bloom, and Gray Wolf again met with Raven's Head.

"You have learned much in the past year," said the wise elder. "Have you also found the very important person you were told to search for?"

Sadly, Gray Wolf said that even now he did not feel much closer to finding that very important person.

Raven's Head shook his head and said, "You have been looking in the wrong places." Then he whispered to Gray Wolf, "Look closer to home. Look within."

The next day Gray Wolf went to the muskeg, a nearby marsh, to think about what Raven's Head had told him.

Suddenly his thoughts were shattered by a loud, clear call that sounded like, "Who? Who?"

Looking up, Gray Wolf saw an owl perched on top of a stump. When he looked again, it seemed to be Raven's Head standing before him.

18

"You! You!" spoke the shaman, pointing his Talking Stick at the surface of the marsh.

Gray Wolf shook his head and rubbed his eyes. The stump, the owl, and the shaman were no longer there! Was his mind playing tricks? Had it all been a dream?

Looking again down into the water, Gray Wolf began to see faces appearing on the surface. First he saw himself, then others.

Gray Wolf turned around but found he was alone! He looked back and saw family, friends, young and old, reflected in the water. It was all the faces of his people. "What does this mean?" he asked out loud.

All at once, Gray Wolf knew he had found what he was looking for. He couldn't wait to get back to the village to tell Raven's Head he had completed his task.

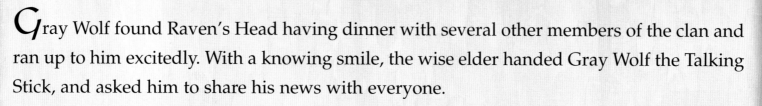

Gray Wolf found Raven's Head having dinner with several other members of the clan and ran up to him excitedly. With a knowing smile, the wise elder handed Gray Wolf the Talking Stick, and asked him to share his news with everyone.

Gray Wolf told the people about his conversations with the animals and about his vision.

"After much time," he said, "I have found a very important person and gotten to know this person well. The very important person is you, and you, and you," he said, pointing all around the circle.

"Through all my travels," continued Gray Wolf, "I found that no one is more important than another. Each one of us is a very important person."

"And you," said Raven's Head to Gray Wolf, "are also a very important person, for you have brought this wisdom to us."

The shaman's words made Gray Wolf feel truly special. He was grateful for what he had learned from his brothers and sisters, the animals in the woods and waters. Feeling older and wiser, he knew there were many more wonderful and important discoveries waiting for him in his future.

24